Mrs. Moskowitz and the Sabbath Candlesticks

Written and illustrated by **AMY SCHWARTZ**

The Jewish Publication Society of America   PHILADELPHIA   5744 · 1983

For Beth and Janet

Library of Congress Cataloging in Publication Data

Schwartz, Amy.
  Mrs. Moskowitz and the Sabbath candlesticks.

  Summary: Mrs. Moskowitz is unhappy in her new
apartment until the discovery of her old Sabbath candlesticks prompts her into a series of activities that turn
her new dwelling into a real home.
  [1. Moving, Household—Fiction.   2. Sabbath—Fiction.
3. Jews—Fiction]   I. Title.
PZ7.S406Mr   1983   [E]   83-17490
ISBN 0-8276-0231-6

Designed by Adrianne Onderdonk Dudden

The moving man set down the last box in Mrs. Moskowitz's new apartment and wiped his brow.

"That's it ma'am," he said. "Enjoy your new home."

Fragile

Mrs. Moskowitz let her cat out of his box.

"You call this a home, Fred?"

She walked through the kitchen and the bedroom and back to the livingroom.

"I miss my old house," she said as she sat down. "I miss the flowers in the front. I miss the porch in the back. I miss the old bathtub where I used to wash Sophie and Sam when they were small.

"This apartment will never be a home."

When Mrs. Moskowitz's son came by that evening, the boxes were still unpacked. Sam kissed his mother and handed her a package.

"I found this in the basement when I was locking up the old house, Mother. You must have forgotten it."

Mrs. Moskowitz shook the box. Then she opened the lid and took out a sack made of soft, white cloth. She untied the sack and pulled out two tarnished candlesticks.

"My Sabbath candlesticks!

"When you were little, Sam, I polished these until you could see yourself in the reflection. For *Shabbat* I cleaned the whole house till it sparkled.

"Sam, remember how good the freshly baked *ḥallah* smelled? Remember the laughing and singing after supper? Remember how happy we were?"

"Yes," Sam said. "I remember."

Mrs. Moskowitz shook her head. "What memories, Sam, what memories."

The next morning, when Mrs. Moskowitz pulled back the curtains, a ray of sunlight struck the candlesticks.

"Look at that, Fred! Aren't they lovely?"

When Mrs. Moskowitz did her marketing, she dropped a jar of silver polish in her basket.

After lunch, Mrs. Moskowitz polished the candlesticks. She held Fred up to them. "Can you see yourself, Fred?"

Then she frowned.

"It's that table, Fred! How can my beautiful candlesticks stand on such a plain table?"

Mrs. Moskowitz climbed about the many boxes piled on the floor.
She tugged at the top flap of the biggest box until it sprang open.

She pulled out a dozen sheets, a blue blanket, and a fluffy
comforter with feathers coming out at the seams, but she didn't
find what she was looking for.

"Oh Fred, where could it be?" Mrs. Moskowitz muttered as she tucked the comforter into the bed.

She rummaged around in the box again. "It's . . . here . . . somewhere . . . here it is!"

Mrs. Moskowitz pulled out a white tablecloth with silver threads dancing around its border.

She shook out the tablecloth and laid it on the table.

"Fred, come look! It's magnificent!"

Mrs. Moskowitz stood back and looked too.

"But Fred," she said, "how can such beautiful candlesticks,
on such a lovely table, stand on such a filthy floor?
Where did I put my mop?"

Mrs. Moskowitz unpacked one box after another and finally found her bucket and mop.

She scrubbed and mopped the livingroom floor, the bedroom floor, and then she cleaned the kitchen.

She washed the kitchen cabinets . . .

and pushed the furniture into place.

Mrs. Moskowitz rubbed her back. "What those candlesticks are putting me through," she groaned. Then she yawned and turned out the light.

In the morning, Mrs. Moskowitz got up early. She watched the
light playing on the candlesticks as she brushed her hair.

"What this table needs is a bunch of flowers, don't you think,
Fred?"

Mrs. Moskowitz put on her hat and coat and walked to the cor-
ner. She went into the flower shop and bought a bunch of posies
and daisies.

On her way home, Mrs. Moskowitz stopped at the grocery store. She bought flour, eggs, yeast, and a box of long white candles. At another store she bought a tall bottle of red wine.

When she got home Mrs. Moskowitz unpacked her groceries.

"A table with *Shabbat* candlesticks, a beautiful tablecloth, and such lovely flowers—it's still missing one thing," she said.

Mrs. Moskowitz found her old tin recipe box and pulled out a worn card.

"Freshly baked *ḥallah*, that's what we need."

Mrs. Moskowitz sifted and stirred and kneaded the dough. Then she rolled it into three long rolls and braided them together.

As she worked, Mrs. Moskowitz thought about baking *hallah* with her mother many years ago. She thought about raising her family in the old house. And she thought about the years still to come.

Mrs. Moskowitz put the two loaves of *ḥallah* in a shallow blue dish and put them aside to rise. Then she wiped her hands on her apron.

"Just one more thing, Fred."

Mrs. Moskowitz went to the phone and called her son.

"Come over tonight, Sam, and bring the family. We'll light the candles and have a Sabbath meal. I'll call Sophie and invite her too."

Then Mrs. Moskowitz lay down for a little nap.

Just before sundown, Sam and his family and Sophie arrived at the door.

"Shabbat shalom!" Sam said as he walked in. "Why mother, just look at this apartment!"

Mrs. Moskowitz picked up Fred. She looked around her.

The boxes were all unpacked. Everything was clean and in place.

The candlesticks stood shining on the table. The apartment looked

beautiful and here was the family to celebrate *Shabbat*.

Mrs. Moskowitz laughed.

"Fred, when did all this happen?"

Mrs. Moskowitz turned to her family.

"Shabbat shalom," she said. "And welcome . . . to my home."

The Sabbath

The Sabbath—*Shabbat*—is the Jewish day of rest. It begins each week at sundown on Friday when candles are lit, and ends at nightfall the next day. The Sabbath is greeted with hymns and song. Then the *Kiddush*, a blessing over wine, is recited. In the *Kiddush*, a short section of the Bible is read, recounting how God created the world in six days and rested on the seventh day, the Sabbath, and made it holy. The Rabbis of the Talmud say that whoever recites these few sentences in welcoming the Sabbath becomes a partner with God in the work of creation.

After *Kiddush*, a blessing is said over two braided loaves of bread called ḥallah. Then the Sabbath meal, a joyous family occasion, begins.

Jews who observe the Sabbath do not work from sundown on Friday to nightfall on Saturday. They go to synagogues and temples. They rest, read, study the Bible, and visit family and friends. When they meet, they wish each other a peaceful Sabbath: *"Shabbat shalom."*

Saturday night, when three stars can be seen in the sky, the *Havdalah* is recited, marking the separation between the holy Sabbath and the six "ordinary" days of the week. The *Havdalah* contains blessings over wine, over the light of a candle, and the aroma of spices. The wine cup for the *Havdalah* service is always filled until it just overflows, in the hope that the week ahead will overflow with blessings.